The Lover's Watch

The Lover's Watch

Or

The Art of Making Love

Aphra Behn

ET REMOTISSIMA PROPE

Hesperus Classics

Hesperus Classics
Published by Hesperus Press Limited
4 Rickett Street, London sw6 1ru
www.hesperuspress.com

First published in 1686
First published by Hesperus Press Limited, 2004

Designed and typeset by Fraser Muggeridge
Printed in the United Arab Emirates by Oriental Press

isbn: 1-84391-074-8

CONTENTS

The Lover's Watch[1]

Sir,

When I had ended this little unlaboured piece, the Watch, *I resolved to dedicate it to someone whom I could fancy the nearest approached the charming Damon. Many fine gentlemen I had in view, of wit and beauty; but still, through their education or a natural propensity to debauchery, I found those virtues wanting that should complete that delicate character Iris gives her lover; and which, at first thought of you, I found centred there to perfection.*

Yes, sir, I found you had all the youth of Damon, without the forward noisy confidence which usually attends your sex. You have all the attracting beauty of my young hero; all that can charm the fair, without the affectation of those that set out for conquests (though you make a thousand without knowing it or the vanity of believing it). You have our Damon's wit with all his agreeable modesty: two virtues that rarely shine together; and the last makes you conceal the noble sallies of the first, with that industry and care you would an amour. And you would no more boast of either of these than of your undoubted bravery.

You are (like our lover too) so discreet that the bashful maid may, without fear of blushing, venture the soft confession of the soul with you; reposing the dear secret in yours with more safety than with her own thoughts. You have all the sweetness of youth, with the sobriety and prudence of age. You have all the power of the gay vices of man, but the angel in your mind has subdued you to the virtues of a god! And all the vicious and industrious examples of the roving wits of the mad town have only served to give you the greater abhorrence to lewdness. And you look down with contempt and pity on that wretched unthinking number who pride themselves in their mean victories over little hearts, and boast their common prizes with that vanity that declares them capable of no higher than that of the ruin of some credulous unfortunate. And no glory like that of the discovery of the brave achievement over the next bottle, to the fool that shall applaud them.

How does the generosity and sweetness of your disposition despise these false entertainments that turn the noble passion of love into ridicule and man into brute!

Methinks I could form another Watch (that should remain a pattern to succeeding ages) how divinely you pass your more sacred hours, how nobly and usefully you divide your time – in which no precious minute is lost, not one glides idly by, but all turns to wondrous account. And all your life is one continued course of virtue and honour. Happy the parents that have the glory to own you! Happy the man that has the honour of your friendship! But oh! How much more happy the fair she for whom you shall sigh! Which, surely, can never be in vain.

There will be such a purity in your flame: all you ask will be so chaste and noble, and uttered with a voice so modest and a look so charming as must, by a gentle force, compel that heart to yield that knows the true value of wit, beauty and virtue.

Since, then, in all the excellencies of mind and body (where no one grace is wanting) you so resemble the all-perfect Damon, suffer me to dedicate this Watch to you.

4

It brings you nothing but rules for love, delicate as your thoughts and innocent as your conversation. And possibly it is the only virtue of the mind you are not perfectly master of, the only noble mystery of the soul you have not yet studied. And though they are rules for every hour, you will find they will neither rob heaven nor your friends of their due – those so valuable devoirs of your life. They will teach you love, but love so pure and so devout that you may mix it even with your religion; and, I know, your fine mind can admit of no other. Whenever the god enters there (fond and wanton as he is, full of arts and guiles) he will be reduced to that native innocence that made him so adored before inconstant man corrupted his divinity and made him wild and wandering. How happy will Iris' Watch be to inspire such a heart! How honoured under the patronage of so excellent a man! Whose wit will credit, whose goodness will defend it, and whose noble and virtuous qualities so justly merit the character Iris has given Damon! And which is believed so very much your due by, sir,

Your most obliged and most humble servant,

A. Behn

THE ARGUMENT

It is in the most happy and august Court of the best and greatest monarch of the world that Damon, a young nobleman whom we will render under that name, languishes for a maid of quality who will give us leave to call her Iris.

Their births are equally illustrious, they are both rich and both young, their beauty such as I do not too nicely particularise, lest I should discover (which I am not permitted to do) who these charming lovers are. Let it suffice that Iris is the most fair and accomplished person that ever adorned a court, and that Damon is only worthy of the glory of her favour, for he has all that can render him lovely in the fair eyes of the amiable Iris. Nor is he master of those superficial beauties alone, that please at first sight; he can charm the soul with a thousand arts of wit and gallantry. And, in a word, I may say, without flattering either, that there is no one beauty, no one grace, no perfection of mind and body, that wants to complete a victory on both sides.

The agreement of age, fortunes, quality and humours in these two fair lovers, made the impatient Damon hope that nothing would oppose his passion, and if he saw himself every hour languishing for the adorable maid, he did not however despair. And if Iris sighed, it was not for fear of being one day more happy.

In the midst of the tranquillity of these two lovers, Iris was obliged to go into the country for some months, whither it was impossible for Damon to wait on her, he being obliged to attend the King his master, and being the most amorous of his sex, suffered with extreme impatience the absence of his mistress. Nevertheless, he failed not to send to her every day, and gave up all his melancholy hours to thinking, sighing, and writing to her the softest letters that love could inspire. So that Iris even blessed that absence that gave her so tender and convincing proofs of his passion, and found this dear way of conversing even recompensed all her sighs for his absence.

After a little intercourse of this kind, Damon bethought himself to ask Iris a discretion which he had won of her before she left the town, and in a billet-doux to that purpose, pressed her very earnestly for it. Iris being infinitely pleased with his importunity, suffered him to ask it often, and he never failed of doing so.

But as I do not here design to relate the adventures of these two amiable persons, nor give you all the billets-doux that passed between them, you shall here find nothing but the watch this charming maid sent her impatient lover.

IRIS TO DAMON

It must be confessed, Damon, that you are the most importuning man in the world. Your billets have a hundred times demanded a discretion which you won of me; and tell me, will you not wait my return to be paid? You are either a very faithless creditor, or believe me very unjust, that you dun[2] with such impatience.

But to let you see that I am a maid of honour, and value my word, I will acquit myself of this obligation I have to you, and send you a watch of my fashion; perhaps you never saw any so good. It is not one of those that have always something to be mended in it, but one that is without fault, very just and good, and will remain so as long as you continue to love me. But, Damon, know that the very minute you cease to do so, the string will break and it will go no more. It is only useful in my absence, and when I return it will change its motion, and though I have set it but for the springtime, it will serve you the whole year round and it will be necessary only that you alter the business of the hours (which my Cupid, in the middle of my watch, points you out) according to the length of the days and nights. Nor is the dart of that little god directed to those hours, so much to inform you how they pass, as how you ought to pass them; how you ought to employ those of your absence from Iris. It is there you shall find the whole business of a lover – from his mistress – for I have designed it a rule to all your actions. The consideration of the workman ought to make you set a value upon the work. And though it be not an accomplished and perfect piece, yet Damon, you ought to be grateful and esteem it, since I have made it for you alone. But however I may boast of the design, I know, as well as I believe you love me, that you will not suffer me to have the glory of it wholly, but will say in your heart,

That Love, the great instructor of the mind,
That forms anew, and fashions every soul,
Refines the gross defects of humankind;
Humbles the proud and vain, inspires the dull;
Gives cowards noble heat in fight,
And teaches feeble women how to write:
That doth the universe command,
Does from my Iris' heart direct her hand.

I give you the liberty to say this to your heart, if you please. And that you may know with what justice you do so, I will confess in my turn.

The Confession

That love's my conduct where I go,
And love instructs me all I do.
Prudence no longer is my guide,
Nor take I counsel of my pride.
In vain does honour now invade,
In vain does reason take my part,
If against love it do persuade,
If it rebel against my heart.
If the soft evening do invite,
And I incline to take the air,
The birds, the spring, the flowers no more delight;
'Tis love makes all the pleasure there:
Love, which about me still I bear;
I'm charmed with what I thither bring,
And add a softness to the spring.
If for devotion I design,
Love meets me, even at the shrine;
In all my worship claims a part,
And robs even heaven of my heart:
All day does counsel and control,
And all the night employs my soul.
No wonder then if all you think be true,
That love's concerned in all I do for you.

And, Damon, you know that Love is no ill master, and I must say, with a blush, that he has found me no unapt scholar, and he instructs too agreeably not to succeed in all he undertakes.

Who can resist his soft commands?
When he resolves, what god withstands?

But I ought to explain to you my watch: the naked Love which you will find in the middle of it, with his wings clipped to show you he is fixed and constant, and will not fly away, points you out with his arrow the four and twenty hours that compose the day and the night. Over every hour you will find written what you ought to do during its course, and every half-hour is marked with a sigh, since the quality of a lover is to sigh day and night. Sighs are the children of lovers that are born every hour. And that my watch may always be just, Love himself ought to conduct it, and your heart should keep time with the movement:

My present's delicate and new,
If by your heart the motion's set;
According as that's false or true,
You'll find my watch will answer it.

Every hour is tedious to a lover separated from his mistress; and to show you how good I am, I will have my watch instruct you to pass some of them without inquietude, that the force of your imagination may sometimes charm the trouble you have for my absence:

Perhaps I am mistaken here,
My heart may too much credit give:
But, Damon, you can charm my fear,
And soon my error undeceive.

But I will not disturb my repose at this time with a jealousy which I hope is altogether frivolous and vain, but begin to instruct you in the mysteries of my watch. Cast then your eyes upon the eighth hour in the morning, which is the hour I would have you begin to wake. You will find there written,

EIGHT O'CLOCK
Agreeable Reverie

Do not rise yet; you may find thoughts agreeable enough when you awake to entertain you longer in bed. And it is in that hour you ought to recollect all the dreams you had in the night. If you had dreamt anything to my advantage, confirm yourself in that thought, but if to my disadvantage, renounce it, and disown the injurious dream. It is in this hour also that I give you leave to reflect on all that I have ever said and done that has been most obliging to you, and that gives you the most tender sentiments.

The Reflections

Remember, Damon, while your mind
Reflects on things that charm and please,
You give me proofs that you are kind,

And set my doubting soul at ease:
For when your heart receives with joy
The thoughts of favours which I give,
My smiles in vain I not employ,
And on the square we love and live.

Think then on all I ever did,
That e'er was charming, e'er was dear;
Let nothing from that soul be hid,
Whose griefs and joys I feel and share.
All that your love and faith have sought,
All that your vows and sighs have bought,
Now render present to your thought.

And for what's to come, I give you leave, Damon, to flatter yourself, and to expect I shall still pursue those methods, whose remembrance charms so well. But if it be possible, conceive these kind thoughts between sleeping and waking, that all my too forward complaisance[3], my goodness, and my tenderness, which I confess to have for you, may pass for half dreams, for it is most certain,

That though the favours of the fair
Are ever to the lover dear;
Yet, lest he should reproach that easy flame,
That buys its satisfaction with its shame;
She ought but rarely to confess
How much she finds of tenderness;
Nicely to guard the yielding part,
And hide the hard-kept secret in her heart.

For let me tell you, Damon, though the passion of a woman of honour be ever so innocent, and the lover ever so discreet and honest, her heart feels I know not what of reproach within, at the reflection of any favours she has allowed him. For my part, I never call to mind the least soft or kind word I have spoken to Damon without finding at the same instant my face covered over with blushes, and my heart with sensible pain. I sigh at the remembrance of every touch I have stolen from his hand, and have upbraided my soul, which confesses so much guilty love, as that secret desire of touching him made appear. I am angry at the discovery, though I am pleased at the same time with the satisfaction I take in doing so, and ever disordered at the remembrance of such arguments of too much love. And these unquiet sentiments alone are sufficient to persuade me that our sex cannot be reserved too much. And I have often, on these occasions, said to myself,

The Reserve

Though Damon every virtue have,
With all that pleases in his form,
That can adorn the just and brave,
That can the coldest bosom warm;
Though wit and honour there abound,
Yet the pursuer's ne'er pursued,
And when my weakness he has found,
His love will sink to gratitude:
While on the asking part he lives,
'Tis she th' obliger is who gives.

And he that at one throw the stake has won
Gives over play, since all the stock is gone.
And what dull gamester ventures certain store
With losers who can set no more?

NINE O'CLOCK
Design to Please Nobody

I should continue to accuse you of that vice I have often done, that of laziness, if you remained past this hour in bed. It is time for you to rise; my watch tells you it is nine o'clock. Remember that I am absent, therefore do not take too much pains in dressing yourself and setting your person off.

The Question

Tell me! What can he design,
Who in his mistress' absence will be fine?
Why does he cock, and comb, and dress?
Why is his cravat string in print?
What does the embroidered coat confess?
Why to the glass this long address,
If there be nothing in't?
If no new conquest is designed,
If no new beauty fill his mind?
Let fools and fops, whose talents lie
In being neat, in being spruce,
Be dressed in vain, and tawdry;
With men of sense, 'tis out of use:

The only folly that distinction sets
Between the noisy fluttering fools and wits.
Remember, Iris is away;
And sighing to your valet cry,
'Spare your perfumes and care today,
I have no business to be gay,
Since Iris is not by.
I'll be all negligent in dress,
And scarce set off for complaisance;
Put me on nothing that may please,
But only such as may give no offence.'

Say to yourself, as you are dressing, 'Would it please Heaven that I might see Iris today! But oh! 'tis impossible. Therefore all that I shall see will be but indifferent objects, since 'tis Iris only that I wish to see.' And sighing, whisper to yourself:

The Sigh

Ah! charming object of my wishing thought!
Ah! soft idea of a distant bliss!
That only art in dreams and fancy brought,
That give short intervals of happiness.
But when I waking find thou absent art,
And with thee, all that I adore,
What pains, what anguish fills my heart!
What sadness seizes me all o'er!
All entertainments I neglect,
Since Iris is no longer there:
Beauty scarce claims my bare respect,

Since in the throng I find not her.
Ah then! how vain it were to dress, and show;
Since all I wish to please is absent now!

It is with these thoughts, Damon, that your mind ought to be employed during your time of dressing. And you are too knowing in love to be ignorant,

That when a lover ceases to be blessed
With the object he desires,
Ah! how indifferent are the rest!
How soon their conversation tires!
Though they a thousand arts to please invent,
Their charms are dull, their wit impertinent.

TEN O'CLOCK
Reading of Letters

My Cupid points you now the hour in which you ought to retire into your cabinet, having already passed an hour in dressing. And for a lover who is sure not to appear before his mistress, even that hour is too much to be so employed.

But I will think you thought of nothing less than dressing while you were about it. Lose then no more minutes, but open your scrutore[4], and read over some of those billets you have received from me. Oh! what pleasures a lover feels about his heart in reading those from a mistress he entirely loves!

The Joy

Who, but a lover, can express
The joys, the pants, the tenderness,
That the soft amorous soul invades,
While the dear billet-doux he reads?
Raptures divine the heart o'erflow,
Which he that loves not cannot know.

A thousand tremblings, thousand fears,
The short-breathed sighs, the joyful tears!
The transport, where the love's confessed;
The change, where coldness is expressed;
The differing flames the lover burns,
As those are shy, or kind, by turns.

However you find them, Damon, construe them all to my advantage. Possibly, some of them have an air of coldness, something different from that softness they are usually too amply filled with; but where you find they have, believe there that the sense of honour, and my sex's modesty, guided my hand a little against the inclinations of my heart; and that it was as a kind of an atonement I believed I ought to make, for something I feared I had said too kind, and too obliging before. But wherever you find that stop, that check in my career of love, you will be sure to find something that follows it to favour you, and deny that unwilling imposition upon my heart; which, lest you should mistake, Love shows himself in smiles again, and flatters more agreeably, disdaining the tyranny of honour and rigid custom, that imposition upon our sex;

and will, in spite of me, let you see he reigns absolutely in my soul.

The reading my billets-doux may detain you an hour. I have had so much goodness to write you enough to entertain you so long at least, and sometimes reproach myself for it, but, contrary to all my scruples, I find myself disposed to give you those frequent marks of my tenderness. If yours be so great as you express it, you ought to kiss my letters a thousand times; you ought to read them with attention, and weigh every word and value every line. A lover may receive a thousand endearing words from a mistress more easily than a billet. One says a great many kind things of course to a lover, which one is not willing to write, or to give testified under one's hand, signed and sealed. But when once a lover has brought his mistress to that degree of love, he ought to assure himself she loves not at the common rate.

Love's Witness

Slight unpremeditated words are borne
By every common wind into the air;
Carelessly uttered, die as soon as born,
And in one instant give both hope and fear:
Breathing all contraries with the same wind,
According to the caprice of the mind.

But billets-doux are constant witnesses,
Substantial records to eternity;
Just evidence, who the truth confess,
On which the lover safely may rely;

They're serious thoughts, digested and resolved;
And last, when words are into clouds devolved.

I will not doubt but you give credit to all that is kind in my letters; and I will believe you find a satisfaction in the entertainment they give you, and that the hour of reading them is not disagreeable to you. I could wish your pleasure might be extreme, even to the degree of suffering the thought of my absence not to diminish any part of it. And I could wish too, at the end of your reading, you would sigh with pleasure, and say to yourself,

The Transport

O Iris! While you thus can charm,
While at this distance you can wound and warm;
My absent torments I will bless and bear,
That give me such dear proofs how kind you are.
Present, the valued store was only seen,
Nor am I rifling the bright mass within.

Every dear, past, and happy day,
When languishing at Iris' feet I lay;
When all my prayers and all my tears could move
No more than her permission I should love:
Vain with my glorious destiny,
I thought, beyond, scarce any heaven could be.

But, charming maid, now I am taught,
That absence has a thousand joys to give,
On which the lovers present never thought,

That recompense the hours we grieve.
Rather by absence let me be undone,
Than forfeit all the pleasures that has won.

With this little rapture, I wish you would finish the reading my letters, shut your scrutore, and quit your cabinet; for my love leads to eleven o'clock.

ELEVEN O'CLOCK
The Hour to Write in

If my watch did not inform you it is now time to write, I believe, Damon, your heart would, and tell you also that I should take it kindly if you would employ a whole hour that way; and that you should never lose an occasion of writing to me, since you are assured of the welcome I give your letters. Perhaps you will say an hour is too much, and that it is not the mode to write long letters. I grant you, Damon, when we write those indifferent ones of gall-antry in course, or necessary compliment; the handsome comprising of which in the fewest words renders them the most agreeable. But in love we have a thousand foolish things to say, that of themselves bear no great sound, but have a mighty sense in love, for there is a peculiar eloquence natural alone to a lover, and to be understood by no other creature. To those, words have a thousand graces and sweetnesses, which to the unconcerned appear meanness[5] and easy sense at the best. But, Damon, you and I are none of those ill judges of the beauties of love; we can penetrate beyond the vulgar, and perceive the fine soul in every line, through all the humble dress of phrase; when possibly they who think they discern it best in florid language do not see it at all. Love was not born or bred in courts, but cottages; and, nursed in groves and shades, smiles on the plains, and wantons in the streams; all unadored and harmless. Therefore, Damon, do not consult your wit in this affair, but Love alone; speak all that he and Nature taught you, and let the fine things you learn in schools alone. Make use of those flowers you have gathered there, when you conversed with statesmen and the gown. Let Iris possess your heart in all its simple innocence; that's the best eloquence to her that loves, and that is my instruction to a lover who would succeed in his amours; for I have a heart very difficult to please, and this is the nearest way to it.

Advice to Lovers

Lovers, if you would gain the heart
Of Damon, learn to win the prize;
He'll show you all its tenderest part,
And where its greatest danger lies;
The magazine of its disdain,
Where honour, feebly guarded, does remain.

If present, do but little say;
Enough the silent lover speaks:
But wait, and sigh, and gaze all day;
Such rhetoric more than language takes.
For words the dullest way do move;
And uttered more to show your wit than love.

Let your eyes tell her of your heart;
Its story is, for words, too delicate.
Souls thus exchange, and thus impart,
And all their secrets can relate.
A tear, a broken sigh, she'll understand;
Or the soft trembling pressings of the hand.

Or if your pain must be in words expressed,
Let 'em fall gently, unassured, and slow;
And where they fail, your looks may tell the rest:
Thus Damon spoke, and I was conquered so.
The witty talker has mistook his art;
The modest lover only charms the heart.

Thus, while all day you gazing sit,
And fear to speak, and fear your fate,
You more advantages by silence get,
Than the gay forward youth with all his prate.
Let him be silent here; but when away,
Whatever love can dictate, let him say.

There let the bashful soul unveil,
And give a loose to love and truth:
Let him improve the amorous tale,
With all the force of words, and fire of youth:
There all, and anything let him express;
Too long he cannot write, too much confess.

O Damon! How well have you made me understand this soft pleasure! You know my tenderness too well not to be sensible how I am charmed with your agreeable long letters.

23

The Invention

Ah! he who first found out the way
Souls to each other to convey,
Without dull speaking, sure must be
Something above humanity.
Let the fond world in vain dispute,
And the first sacred mystery impute
Of letters to the learned brood,
And of the glory cheat a god:
'Twas Love alone that first the art essayed,
And Psyche was the first fair yielding maid,
That was by the dear billets-doux betrayed.

It is an art too ingenious to have been found out by man, and too necessary to lovers not to have been invented by the god of love himself. But, Damon, I do not pretend to exact from you those letters of gallantry which, I have told you, are filled with nothing but fine thoughts, and written with all the arts of wit and subtlety. I would have yours still all tender unaffected love, words unchosen, thoughts unstudied, and love unfeigned. I had rather find more softness than wit in your passion; more of nature than of art; more of the lover than the poet.

Nor would I have you write any of those little short letters that are read over in a minute; in love, long letters bring a long pleasure. Do not trouble yourself to make them fine, or write a great deal of wit and sense in a few lines; that is the notion of a witty billet, in any affair but that of love. And have a care rather to avoid these graces to a mistress, and assure yourself, dear Damon, that what pleases the soul pleases the eye, and the largeness or bulk of your letter shall never offend me; and that I only am displeased when I find them small. A letter is ever the best and most powerful agent to a mistress; it almost always persuades, it is always renewing little impressions that possibly otherwise absence would deface. Make use then, Damon, of your time while it is given you, and thank me that I permit you to write to me. Perhaps I shall not always continue in the humour of suffering you to do so, and it may so happen, by some turn of chance and fortune, that you may be deprived at the same time both of my presence and of the means of sending to me. I will believe that such an accident would be a great misfortune to you, for I have often heard you say that, 'To make the most happy lover suffer martyrdom, one need only forbid him seeing, speaking and writing to the object he loves.' Take all the advantages then you can; you cannot give me too often marks too powerful of your passion. Write therefore during this hour, every day. I give you leave to believe that while you do so, you are serving me the most obligingly and agreeably you can while absent; and that you are giving me a remedy against all grief, uneasiness, melancholy, and despair; nay, if you exceed your hour, you need not be ashamed. The time you employ in this kind devoir is the time that I shall be grateful for, and no doubt will recompense it. You ought not, however, to neglect heaven for me; I will give you time for your devotion, for my watch tells you it is time to go to the temple.

TWELVE O'CLOCK
Indispensable Duty

There are certain duties which one ought never to neglect. That of adoring the gods is of this nature, and which we ought to pay from the bottom of our hearts. And that, Damon, is the only time I will dispense with your not thinking on me. But I would not have you go to one of those temples where the celebrated beauties and those that make a profession of gallantry go; and who come thither only to see and be seen; and whither they repair more to show their beauty and dress than to honour the gods. If you will take my advice and oblige my wish, you shall go to those that are least frequented, and you shall appear there like a man that has a perfect veneration for all things sacred.

The Instruction

Damon, if your heart and flame,
You wish, should always be the same,
Do not give it leave to rove,
Nor expose it to new harms:
Ere you think on't, you may love,
If you gaze on beauty's charms:
If with me you would not part,
Turn your eyes into your heart.

If you find a new desire
In your easy soul take fire,
From the tempting ruin fly;
Think it faithless, think it base:
Fancy soon will fade and die,
If you wisely cease to gaze.
Lovers should have honour too,
Or they pay but half love's due.

Do not to the temple go,
With design to gaze or show:
Whate'er thoughts you have abroad,
Though you can deceive elsewhere,
There's no feigning with your God;
Souls should be all perfect there.
The heart that's to the altar brought,
Only Heaven should fill its thought.

Do not your sober thoughts perplex,
By gazing on the ogling sex:
Or if beauty call your eyes,
Do not on the object dwell;
Guard your heart from the surprise,
By thinking Iris doth excel.
Above all earthly things I'd be,
Damon, most beloved by thee;
And only Heaven must rival me.

I perceive it will be very difficult to you to quit the temple without being surrounded with compliments from people of ceremony, friends, and newsmongers, and several of those sorts of persons who afflict and busy themselves and rejoice at a hundred things they have no interest in; coquettes and politicians who make it the business of their whole lives to gather all the news of the town; adding or diminishing according to the stock of their wit and invention, and spreading it all abroad to the believing fools and gossips, and perplexing everybody with a hundred ridiculous novels, which they pass off for wit and entertainment. Or else some of those recounters of adventures that are always telling of intrigues, and that make a secret to a hundred people of a thousand foolish things they have heard. Like a certain pert and impertinent lady of the town, whose youth and beauty being past, set up for wit to uphold a feeble empire over hearts, and whose character is this:

The Coquette

Melinda, who had never been
Esteemed a beauty at fifteen,
Always amorous was, and kind:
To every swain she lent an ear;
Free as air, but false as wind;
Yet none complained, she was severe.
She eased more than she made complain;
Was always singing, pert, and vain.

Where'er the throng was, she was seen,
And swept the youths along the green;
With equal grace she flattered all;
And fondly proud of all address,
Her smiles invite, her eyes do call,
And her vain heart her looks confess.
She rallies this, to that she bowed,
Was talking ever, laughing loud.

On every side she makes advance,
And everywhere a confidence;
She tells for secrets all she knōws,
And all to know she does pretend:
Beauty in maids she treats as foes:
But every handsome youth as friend.
Scandal still passes off for truth;
And noise and nonsense, wit and youth.

Coquette all o'er, and every part,
Yet wanting beauty, even of art;
Herds with the ugly and the old;
And plays the critic on the rest:
Of men, and bashful, and the bold,
Either, and all, by turns, likes best:
Even now, though youth be languished, she
Sets up for love and gallantry.

This sort of creature, Damon, is very dangerous; not that I fear you will squander away a heart upon her, but your hours; for in spite of you, she'll detain you with a thousand impertinencies, and eternal tattle. She passes for a judging wit; and there is nothing so troublesome as such a pretender. She perhaps may get some knowledge of our correspondence, and then, no doubt, will improve it to my disadvantage. Possibly she may rail at me; that is her fashion by the way of friendly speaking; and an awkward commendation the most effectual way of defaming and traducing. Perhaps she tells you, in a cold tone, that you are a happy man to be beloved by me. That Iris indeed is handsome, and she wonders she has no more lovers; but the men are not of her mind; if they were, you should have more rivals. She commends my face, but that I have blue eyes, and it is pity my complexion is no better. My shape but too much inclining to fat. Cries: 'She would charm infinitely with her wit, but that she knows too well she is mistress of it;' and concludes, 'But all together she is well enough.' Thus she runs on without giving you leave to edge in a word in my defence, and ever and anon crying up her own conduct and management. Tells you how she is oppressed with lovers and fatigued with addresses, and recommending herself, at every turn, with a perceivable cunning. And all the while is jilting you of your good opinion, which she would buy at the price of anybody's repose, or her own fame, though but for the vanity of adding to the number of her lovers. When she sees a new spark, the first thing she does, she enquires into his estate. If she find it such as may (if the coxcomb be well managed) supply her vanity, she makes advances to him, and applies herself to all those little arts she usually makes use of to gain her fools, and according to his humour dresses and affects her own. But, Damon, since I point to no particular person in this character, I will not name who you should avoid, but all of this sort I conjure you, wheresoever you find them. But if unlucky chance throw you in their way, hear all they say, without credit or regard, as far as decency will suffer you; hear them without approving their foppery, and hear them without giving them cause to censure you. But it is so much lost time to listen to all the novels this sort of people will perplex you with; whose business is to be idle, and who even tire themselves with their own impertinencies. And be assured after all there is nothing they can tell you that is worth your knowing. And, Damon, a perfect lover never asks any news but of the maid he loves.

The Enquiry

Damon, if your love be true
To the heart that you possess,
Tell me what have you to do
Where you have no tenderness?
Her affairs, who cares to learn,
For whom he has not some concern?

If a lover fain would know
If the object loved be true,
Let her but industrious be
To watch his curiosity;
Though ne'er so cold his questions seem,
They come from warmer thoughts within.

When I hear a swain enquire
What gay Melinda does to live,
I conclude there is some fire
In a heart inquisitive;
Or 'tis, at least, the bill that's set
To show the heart is to be let.

TWO O'CLOCK
Dinner Time

Leave all those fond entertainments, or you will disoblige
me and make dinner wait for you, for my Cupid tells you it
is that hour. Love does not pretend to make you lose that,
nor is it my province to order you your diet. Here I give
you a perfect liberty to do what you please; and possibly it
is the only hour in the whole four and twenty that I will
absolutely resign you, or dispense with your even so much
as thinking on me. It is true, in seating yourself at table,
I would not have you placed over against a very beautiful
object; for in such a one there are a thousand little graces
in speaking, looking and laughing, that fail not to charm,
if one gives way to the eyes, to gaze and wander that way,
in which perhaps, in spite of you, you will find a pleasure.
And while you do so, though without design or concern,
you give the fair charmer a sort of vanity in believing
you have placed yourself there, only for the advantage of
looking on her; and she assumes a hundred little graces
and affectations which are not natural to her, to complete a
conquest which she believes so well begun already. She
softens her eyes, and sweetens her mouth; and, in fine,

puts on another air than when she had no design, and when you did not, by your continual looking on her, rouse her vanity and increase her easy opinion of her own charms. Perhaps she knows I have some interest in your heart, and prides herself, at least, with believing she has attracted the eyes of my lover, if not his heart, and thinks it easy to vanquish the whole if she pleases; and triumphs over me in her secret imaginations. Remember, Damon, that while you act thus in the company and conversation of other beauties, every look or word you give in favour of them is an indignity to my reputation; and which you cannot suffer if you love me truly and with honour. And assure yourself, so much vanity as you inspire in her, so much fame you rob me of, for whatever praises you give another beauty, so much you take away from mine. Therefore, if you dine in company, do as others do. Be generally civil, not applying yourself by words or looks to any particular person. Be as gay as you please. Talk and laugh with all, for this is not the hour for chagrin.

The Permission

My Damon, though I stint your love,
I will not stint your appetite;
That I would have you still improve,
By every new and fresh delight.
Feast till Apollo hides his head,
Or drink the amorous god to Thetis' bed.[6]

Be like yourself: all witty, gay!
And o'er the bottle bless the board;

The listening round will, all the day,
Be charmed, and pleased with every word.
Though Venus' son inspire your wit,
'Tis the Silenian god[7] best utters it.

Here talk of everything but me,
Since everything you say with grace:
If not disposed your humour be,
And you'd this hour in silence pass;
Since something must the subject prove
Of Damon's thoughts, let it be me and love.

But, Damon, this enfranchised hour,
No bounds, or laws, will I impose;
But leave it wholly in your power,
What humour to refuse or choose:
I rules prescribe but to your flame;
For I your mistress, not physician, am.

THREE O'CLOCK
Visits to Friends

Damon, my watch is juster than you imagine; it would not have you live retired and solitary, but permits you to go and make visits. I am not one of those that believe love and friendship cannot find a place in one and the same heart. And that man would be very unhappy who, as soon as he had a mistress, should be obliged to renounce the society of his friends. I must confess, I would not that you should have so much concern for them as you have for me; for

I have heard a sort of a proverb that says, 'He cannot be very fervent in love, who is not a little cold in friendship.' You are not ignorant that when Love establishes himself in a heart, he reigns a tyrant there, and will not suffer even friendship, if it pretend to share his empire there.

Cupid

Love is a god, whose charming sway
Both heaven and earth and seas obey;
A power that will not mingled be
With any dull equality.
Since first from heaven, which gave him birth,
He ruled the empire of the earth;
Jealous of sovereign power he rules,
And will be absolute in souls.

I should be very angry if you had any of those friendships which one ought to desire in a mistress only; for many times it happens that you have sentiments a little too tender for those amiable persons; and many times love and friendship are so confounded together that one cannot easily discern one from the other. I have seen a man flatter himself with an opinion that he had but an esteem for a woman, when by some turn of fortune in her life, as marrying, or receiving the addresses of men, he has found by spite and jealousies within, that that was love which he before took for complaisance or friendship. Therefore have a care, for such amities are dangerous. Not but that a lover may have fair and generous female friends, whom he ought to visit; and perhaps I should esteem you less if I did not believe you were valued by such, if I were perfectly assured they were friends and not lovers. But have a care you hide not a mistress under this veil, or that you gain not a lover by this pretence. For you may begin with friendship, and end with love, and I should be equally afflicted should you give it or receive it. And though you charge our sex with all the vanity, yet I often find nature to have given you as large a portion of that common crime which you would shuffle off as ashamed to own; and are as fond and vain of the imagination of a conquest as any coquette of us all; though at the same time you despise the victim, you think it adds a trophy to your fame. And I have seen a man dress, and trick, and adjust his looks and mien, to make a visit to a woman he loved not, nor ever could love, as for those he made to his mistress; and only for the vanity of making a conquest upon a heart, even unworthy of the little pains he has taken about it. And what is this but buying vanity at the expense of ease; and with fatigue to purchase the name of a conceived fop, besides that of a dishonest man? For he who takes pains to make himself beloved only to please his curious humour – though he should say nothing that tends to it more than by his looks, his sighs, and now and then breaking into praises and commendations of the object – by the care he takes to appear well dressed before her and in good order, he lies in his looks, he deceives with his mien and fashion, and cheats with every motion and every grace he puts on. He cozens[8] when he sings or dances, he dissembles when he sighs, and everything he does that wilfully gains upon her, is malice prepense[9], baseness, and art below a man of sense or virtue, and yet these arts, these cozenages, are the common practices of the town. What's this but that damnable vice of which they so reproach our sex – that of jilting for hearts? And it is in vain that my lover, after such foul play, shall think to appease me with saying he did it to try how easy he could conquer, and of how great force his charms were. And why should I be angry if all the town loved him, since he loved none but Iris? Oh foolish pleasure! How little sense goes to the making of such a happiness! And how little love must he have for one particular person, who would wish to inspire it into all the world, and yet himself pretend to be insensible! But this, Damon, is rather what is but too much practised by your sex, than any guilt I charge on you, though vanity be an ingredient that nature very seldom omits in the composition of either sex, and you may be allowed a tincture of it at least. And, perhaps, I am not wholly exempt from this leven in my nature, but accuse myself sometimes of finding a secret joy of being adored, though I even hate my worshipper. But if any such pleasure touch my heart, I find it at the same time blushing in my cheeks with a guilty shame, which soon checks the petty triumphs; and I have a virtue at soberer thoughts that I find surmounts my weakness and indiscretion, and I hope Damon finds the same. For, should he have any of those attachments, I should have no pity for him.

The Example

Damon, if you'd have me true,
Be you my precedent and guide:
Example sooner we pursue,

37

Than the dull dictates of our pride.
Precepts of virtue are too weak an aim,
'Tis demonstration that can best reclaim.

Show me the path you'd have me go;
With such a guide I cannot stray:
What you approve, whate'er you do,
It is but just I bend the way.
If true, my honour favours your design;
If false, revenge is the result of mine.

A lover true, a maid sincere,
Are to be prized as things divine:
'Tis justice makes the blessing dear,
Justice of love without design.
And she that reigns not in a heart alone
Is never safe, or easy, on her throne.

FOUR O'CLOCK
General Conversation

In this visiting hour, many people will happen to meet at one and the same time together in a place. And as you make not visits to friends to be silent, you ought to enter into conversation with them, but those conversations ought to be general, and of general things, for there is no necessity of making your friend the confident of your amours. It would infinitely displease me to hear you have revealed to them all that I have reposed in you; though secrets ever so trivial, yet since uttered between lovers, they deserve to be prized at a higher rate. For what can show a heart more indifferent and indiscreet than to declare in any fashion, or with mirth, or joy, the tender things a mistress says to a lover, and which possibly, related at second hand, bear not the same sense, because they have not the same sound and air they had originally when they came from the soft heart of her, who sighed them first to her lavish lover? Perhaps they are told again with mirth, or joy, unbecoming their character and business; and then they lose their graces (for love is the most solemn thing in nature, and the most unsuiting with gaiety). Perhaps the soft expressions suit not so well the harsher voice of the masculine lover, whose accents were not formed for so much tenderness; at least, not of that sort. For words that have the same meaning are altered from their sense by the least tone or accent of the voice; and those proper and fitted to my soul are not possibly so to yours, though both have the same efficacy upon us – yours upon my heart, as mine upon yours – and both will be misunderstood by the unjudging world. Besides this, there is a holiness in love that's true that ought not to be profaned. And as the poet truly says, at the latter end of an ode of which I will recite the whole:

The Invitation

Amynta, fear not to confess
The charming secret of thy tenderness:
That which a lover can't conceal,
That which, to me, thou shouldst reveal;
And is but what thy lovely eyes express.

Come, whisper to my panting heart,
That heaves and meets thy voice halfway;
That guesses what thou wouldst impart,
And languishes for what thou hast to say.
Confirm my trembling doubt, and make me know
Whence all these blessings and these sighings flow.

Why dost thou scruple to unfold
A mystery that does my life concern?
If thou ne'er speakst, it will be told;
For lovers all things can discern.
From every look, from every bashful grace,
That still succeed each other in thy face,
I shall the dear transporting secret learn:
But 'tis a pleasure not to be expressed,
To hear it by the voice confessed,
When soft sighs breathe it on my panting breast.

All calm and silent is the grove,
Whose shading boughs resist the day;
Here thou mayst blush and talk of love,
While only winds, unheeding, stay,
That will not bear the sound away:
While I with solemn awful joy
All my attentive faculties employ;
Listening to every valued word;
And in my soul the secret treasure hoard:
There like some mystery divine,
The wondrous knowledge I'll enshrine.
Love can his joys no longer call his own,
Than the dear secret's kept unknown.

There is nothing more true than those two last lines, and that love ceases to be a pleasure when it ceases to be a secret, and one you ought to keep sacred. For the world, which never makes a right judgement of things, will misinterpret love, as they do religion; everyone judging it according to the notion he hath of it or the talent of his sense. 'Love,' as a great duke said, 'is like apparitions; everyone talks of them, but few have seen 'em.' Everybody thinks himself capable of understanding love, and that he is a master in the art of it, when there is nothing so nice or difficult to be rightly comprehended, and indeed cannot be but to a soul very delicate. Nor will he make himself known to the vulgar. There must be an uncommon fineness in the mind that contains him; the rest he only visits in as many disguises as there are dispositions and natures where he makes but a short stay and is gone. He can fit himself to all hearts, being the greatest flatterer in the world. And he possesses everyone with a confidence that they are in the number of his elect; and they think they know him perfectly, when nothing but the spirits refined possess him in his excellency. From this difference of love in different souls proceed those odd fantastic maxims which so many hold of so different kinds. And this makes the most innocent pleasures pass oftentimes for crimes with the unjudging crowd who call themselves lovers. And you will have your passion censured by as many as you shall discover it to, and as many several ways. I advise you therefore, Damon, to make no confidents of your amours; and believe that silence has, with me, the most powerful charm.

It is also in these conversations that those indiscreetly

civil persons often are, who think to oblige a good man, by letting him know he is beloved by someone or other; and making him understand how many good qualities he is master of, to render him agreeable to the fair sex, if he would but advance where love and good fortune call; and that a too constant lover loses a great part of his time, which might be managed to more advantage, since youth hath so short a race to run. This, and a thousand the like indecent complaisances, give him a vanity that suits not with that discretion which has hitherto acquired him so good a reputation. I would not have you, Damon, act on these occasions as many of the easy sparks have done before you, who receive such weakness and flattery for truth; and passing it off with a smile, suffer them to advance in folly till they have gained a credit with them and they believe all they hear; telling them they do so by consenting gestures, silence, or open approbation. For my part, I should not condemn a lover that should answer a sort of civil brokers for Love, somewhat briskly; and by giving them to understand they are already engaged, or directing them to fools that will possibly hearken to them and credit such stuff, shame them out of a folly so infamous and disingenuous. In such a case only I am willing you should own your passion; not that you need tell the object which has charmed you. And you may say you are already a lover, without saying you are beloved. For so long as you appear to have a heart unengaged, you are exposed to all the little arts and addresses of this sort of obliging procurers of love, and give way to the hope they have of making you their proselyte. For your own reputation then, and my ease and honour, shun such conversations; for they are neither creditable to you, nor pleasing to me. And believe me, Damon, a true lover has no curiosity but what concerns his mistress.

FIVE O'CLOCK
Dangerous Visits

I foresee, or fear, that these busy impertinent friends will oblige you to visit some ladies of their acquaintance or yours; my watch does not forbid you. Yet I must tell you, I apprehend danger in such visits; and I fear you will have need of all your care and precaution in these encounters, that you may give me no cause to suspect you. Perhaps you will argue that civility obliges you to it. If I were assured there would no other design be carried on, I should believe it were to advance an amorous prudence too far to forbid you. Only keep yourself upon your guard; for the business of most part of the fair sex is to seek only the conquest of hearts. All their civilities are but so many interests; and they do nothing without design. And in such conversations there is always a *je ne sais quoi* that is feared, especially when beauty is accompanied with youth and gaiety; and which they assume upon all occasions that may serve their turn. And I confess, it is not an easy matter to be just in these hours and conversations. The most certain way of being so is to imagine I read all your thoughts, observe all your looks, and hear all your words.

The Caution

My Damon, if your heart be kind,
Do not too long with beauty stay;
For there are certain moments when the mind
Is hurried by the force of charms away.
In fate a minute critical there lies,
That waits on love, and takes you by surprise.

A lover pleased with constancy,
Lives still as if the maid he loved were by:
As if his actions were in view,
As if his steps she did pursue;
Or that his very soul she knew.
Take heed; for though I am not present there,
My love, my genius waits you everywhere.

I am very much pleased with the remedy you say you
make use of to defend yourself from the attacks that beauty
gives your heart; which in one of your billets, you said was
this, or to this purpose:

The Charm for Constancy

Iris, to keep my soul entire and true,
It thinks, each moment of the day, on you.
And when a charming face I see,
That does all other eyes incline,
It has no influence on me:
I think it ev'n deformed to thine.
My eyes, my soul and sense regardless move

44

To all, but the dear object of my love.

But, Damon, I know all lovers are naturally flatterers, though they do not think so themselves, because everyone makes a sense of beauty according to his own fancy. But perhaps you will say in your own defence that it is not flattery to say an unbeautiful woman is beautiful if he that says so believes she is so. I should be content to acquit you of the first, provided you allow me the last. And if I appear charming in Damon's eyes, I am not fond of the approbation of any other. It is enough the world thinks me not altogether disagreeable to justify his choice; but let your good opinion give what increase it pleases to my beauty – though your approbation give me a pleasure, it shall not a vanity; and I am contented that Damon should think me a beauty, without my believing I am one. It is not to draw new assurances, and new vows from you, that I speak this; though tales of love are the only ones we desire to hear often told, and which never tire the hearers if addressed to themselves. But it is not to this end I now seem to doubt what you say to my advantage. No, my heart knows no disguise, nor can dissemble one thought of it to Damon; it is all sincere, and honest as his wish. It is therefore it tells you it does not credit everything you say; though I believe you say abundance of truths in a great part of my character. But when you advance to that which my own sense, my judgement, or my glass cannot persuade me to believe, you must give me leave either to believe you think me vain enough to credit you, or pleased that your sentiments and mine are differing in this point. But I doubt I may rather reply in some verses a friend of yours and mine sent to a person she thought had but indifferent sentiments for her; yet who nevertheless flattered her, because he imagined she had a very great esteem for him. She is a woman that, you know, naturally hates flattery. On the other side, she was extremely dissatisfied and uneasy at his opinion of his being more in her favour than she desired he should believe. So that one night having left her full of pride and anger, she next morning sent him these verses instead of a billet-doux.

The Defiance

By Heaven 'tis false, I am not vain;
And rather would the subject be
Of your indifference or disdain,
Than wit or raillery.

Take back the trifling praise you give,
And pass it on some easier fool,
Who may the injuring wit believe,
That turns her into ridicule.

Tell her she's witty, fair and gay,
With all the charms that can subdue:
Perhaps she'll credit what you say:
But curse me if I do.

If your diversion you design,
On my good nature you have pressed:
Or if you do intend it mine,
You have mistook the jest.

Philander, fly that guilty art:
Your charming facile wit will find,
It cannot play on any heart,
That is sincere and kind.

For wit with softness to reside,
Good nature is with pity stor'd;
But flattery's the result of pride,
And fawns to be adored.

Nay, even when you smile and bow,
'Tis to be rendered more complete:
Your wit, with every grace you show,
Is but a popular cheat.

Laugh on, and call me coxcomb – do;
And your opinion to improve,
Think all you think of me is true;
And to confirm it, swear I love.

Then, while you wreck my soul with pain,
And of a cruel conquest boast,
'Tis you, Philander, that are vain,
And witty at my cost.

Possibly, the angry Amynta, when she wrote these verses, was more offended that he believed himself beloved than that he flattered; though she would seem to make that a great part of the quarrel and cause of her resentment. For we are often in a humour to seem more modest in that point than naturally we are, being too apt to have a favourable opinion of ourselves. And it is rather the effects of a fear that we are flattered than our own ill opinion of the beauty flattered; and that the praiser thinks not so well of it as we do ourselves, or at least we wish he should. Not but there are grains of allowance for the temper of him that speaks. One man's humour is to talk much and he may be permitted to enlarge upon the praise he gives the person he pretends to without being accused of much guilt. Another hates to be wordy; from such an one I have known one soft expression, one tender thing, go as far as whole days everlasting protestations urged with vows and mighty eloquence. And both the one and the other indeed must be allowed in good manners to stretch the compliment beyond the bounds of nice truth, and we must not wonder to hear a man call a woman a beauty when she is not ugly, or another a great wit if she have but common sense above the vulgar, well bred when well dressed, and good-natured when civil. And as I should be very ridiculous if I took all you said for absolute truth, so I should be very unjust not to allow you very sincere in almost all you said besides, and those things the most material to love – honour and friendship. And for the rest, Damon, be it true or false, this believe; you speak with such a grace that I cannot choose but credit you; and find an infinite pleasure in that faith, because I love you. And if I cannot find the cheat, I am contented you should deceive me on, because you do it so agreeably.

SIX O'CLOCK
Walk without Design

You yet have time to walk, and my watch foresaw you could not refuse your friends. You must to the park, or to the mall, for the season is fair and inviting, and all the young beauties love those places too well not to be there. It is there that a thousand intrigues are carried on, and as many more designed. It is there that everyone is set out for conquest, and who aim at nothing less than hearts. Guard yours well, my Damon, and be not always admiring what you see. Do not, in passing by, sigh them silent praises. Suffer not so much as a guilty wish to approach your thoughts, nor a heedful glance to steal from your fine eyes. Those are regards you ought only to have for her you love. But oh! above all, have a care of what you say. You are not reproachable if you should remain silent all the time of your walk; nor would those that know you believe it the effects of dullness, but melancholy. And if any of your friends ask you, 'Why you are so?' I will give you leave to sigh, and say,

The Malcontent

Ah! wonder not if I appear
Regardless of the pleasures here;
Or that my thoughts are thus confined
To the just limits of my mind.
My eyes take no delight to rove
O'er all the smiling charmers of the grove,
Since she is absent whom they love.

49

Ask me not why the flowery spring,
Or the gay little birds that sing,
Or the young streams no more delight,
Or shades and arbours can't invite.
Why the soft murmurs of the wind,
Within the thick-grown groves confined,
No more my soul transport or cheer;
Since all that's charming – Iris – is not here;
Nothing seems glorious, nothing fair.

Then suffer me to wander thus,
With downcast eyes, and arms across:
Let beauty unregarded go;
The trees and flowers unheeded grow.
Let purling streams neglected glide;
With all the spring's adorning pride.
'Tis Iris only soul can give
To the dull shades, and plains, and make 'em thrive;
Nature and my last joys retrieve.

I do not, for all this, wholly confine your eyes. You may look indifferently on all, but with a particular regard on none. You may praise all the beauties in general, but no single one too much. I will not exact from you neither an entire silence. There are a thousand civilities you ought to pay to all your friends and acquaintances; and while I caution you of actions that may get you the reputation of a lover of some of the fair that haunt those places, I would not have you, by an unnecessary and uncomplaisant sullenness, gain that of a person too negligent or morose. I would have you remiss in no one punctilio of good manners. I would have you very just, and pay all you owe; but in these affairs be not over generous and give away too much. In fine, you may look, speak and walk; but, Damon, do it all without design. And while you do so, remember that Iris sent you this advice.

The Warning

Take heed, my Damon, in the grove,
Where beauties with design do walk;
Take heed, my Damon, how you look and talk,
For there are ambuscades of love.

The very winds that softly blow,
Will help betray your easy heart;
And all the flowers that blushing grow,
The shades about, and rivulets below,
Will take the victor's part.

Remember, Damon, all thy safety lies
In the just conduct of your eyes.
The heart, by nature good and brave,
Is to those treacherous guards a slave.
If they let in the fair destructive foe,

Scarce honour can defend her noble seat:
Ev'n she will be corrupted too,
Or driven to a retreat.
The soul is but the cully to the sight.
And must be pleased in what that takes delight.

Therefore examine yourself well, and conduct your eyes during this walk like a lover that seeks nothing. And do not stay too long in these places.

It is time to be weary, it is night. Take leave of your friends and retire home. It is in this retreat that you ought to recollect in your thoughts all the actions of the day, and all those things that you ought to give me an account of in your letter. You cannot hide the least secret from me without treason against sacred love. For all the world agrees that confidence is one of the greatest proofs of the passion of love; and that lover who refuses his confidence to the person he loves is to be suspected to love but very indifferently, and to think very poorly of the sense and generosity of his mistress. But that you may acquit yourself like a man, and a lover of honour, and leave me no doubt upon my soul, think of all you have done this day, that I may have all the story of it in your next letter to me; but deal faithfully, and neither add nor diminish in your relation; the truth and sincerity of your confession will atone even for little faults that you shall commit against me in some of those things you shall tell me. For if you have failed in any point or circumstance of love, I had much rather hear it from you than another. For it is a sort of repentance to accuse yourself; and would be a crime unpardonable if you suffer me to hear it from any other. And be assured, while you confess it, I shall be indulgent enough to forgive you. The noblest quality of man is sincerity; and, Damon, one ought to have as much of it in love as in any other business of one's life, notwithstanding the most part of men make no account of it there; but will believe there ought to be double-dealing, and an art practised in love as well as in war. But, oh! beware of that notion.

Sincerity

Sincerity! thou greatest good!
Thou virtue which so many boast!
And art so nicely understood!
And often in the searching lost!
For when we do approach thee near,
The fine idea framed of thee,
Appears not now so charming fair
As the most useful flattery.
Thou hast no glittering to invite;
Nor takest the lover at first sight.

The modest virtue shuns the crowd,
And lives, like vestals, in a cell;
In cities 'twill not be allowed,
Nor takes delight in courts to dwell:
'Tis nonsense with the man of wit;
And ev'n a scandal to the great:
For all the young, and fair, unfit;
And scorn'd by wiser fops of state.
A virtue yet was never known
To the false trader, or the falser gown.

And, Damon, though thy noble blood
Be most illustrious, and refined;
Though every grace and every good
Adorn thy person and thy mind:
Yet, if this virtue shine not there,
This godlike virtue, which alone,
Wert thou less witty, brave, or fair,
Would for all these, less prized, atone;
My tender folly I'd control,
And scorn the conquest of thy soul.

EIGHT O'CLOCK
Impatient Demands

After you have sufficiently collected yourself of all the past actions of the day, call your page into your cabinet, or him whom you trusted with your last letter to me; where you ought to enquire of him a thousand things, and all of me. Ask impatiently, and be angry if he answers not your curiosity soon enough. Think that he has a dreaming in his voice, in these moments more than at other times; and reproach him with dullness. For it is most certain that when one loves tenderly, we would know in a minute what cannot be related in an hour. Ask him, how I did? How I received his letter? And if he examined the air of my face, when I took it? If I blushed or looked pale? If my hand trembled, or I spoke to him with short interrupting sighs? If I asked him any questions about you, while I was opening the seal? Or if I could not well speak, and was silent? If I read it attentively, and with joy? And all this, before you open the answer I have sent you by him, which, because you are impatient to read, you, with the more haste and earnestness, demand all you expect from him; and that you may the better know what humour I was in when I wrote that to you. For oh! a lover has a thousand little fears and dreads, he knows not why. In fine, make him recount to you all that passed while he was with me; and then you ought to read that which I have sent, that you may inform yourself of all that passes in my heart, for you may assure yourself all that I say to you that way proceeds from thence.

The Assurance

How shall a lover come to know,
Whether he's beloved or no?
What dear things must she impart,
To assure him of her heart?

Is it when her blushes rise;
And she languish in her eyes;
Tremble when he does approach;
Look pale, and faint at every touch?

Is it, when a thousand ways
She does his wit and beauty praise;
Or she venture to explain,
In less moving words, a pain;
Though so indiscreet she grows,
To confirm it with her vows?

These some short-lived passion moves,
While the object's by, she loves;
While the gay and sudden fire
Kindles by some fond desire:
And a coldness will ensue,
When the lover's out of view.
Then she reflects with scandal o'er
The easy scene that passed before:
Then, with blushes, would recall
The unconsidering criminal;
In which a thousand faults she'll find,
And chide the errors of her mind.
Such fickle weight is found in words,
As no substantial faith affords:
Deceived and baffled all may be,
Who trust that frail security.

But a well-digested flame
That will always be the same;
And that does from merit grow,
Established by our reason too;
By a better way will prove,
'Tis the unerring fire of love.
Lasting records it will give:
And, that all she says may live;
Sacred and authentic stand,
Her heart confirms it by her hand.
If this, a maid, well born, allow;
Damon, believe her just and true.

You will not have much trouble to explain what my watch designs here. There can be no thought more afflicting than that of the absence of a mistress; and which the sighings of the heart will soon make you find. Ten thousand fears oppress him; he is jealous of everybody, and envies those eyes and ears that are charmed by being near the object adored. He grows impatient, and makes a thousand resolutions, and as soon abandons them all. He gives himself wholly up to the torment of uncertainty; and by degrees, from one cruel thought to another, winds himself up to insupportable chagrin. Take this hour then, to think on your misfortunes, which cannot be small to a soul that is wholly sensible of love. And everyone knows that a lover, deprived of the object of his heart, is deprived of all the world, and inconsolable. For though one wishes without ceasing for the dear charmer one loves, and though you speak of her every minute; though you are writing to her every day, and though you are infinitely pleased with the dear and tender answer; yet, to speak sincerely, it must be confessed that the felicity of a true lover is to be always near his mistress. And you may tell me, O Damon!, what you please, and say that absence inspires the flame which perpetual presence would satiate. I love too well to be of that mind, and when I am,I shall believe my passion is declining. I know not whether it advances your love; but surely it must ruin your repose. And it is impossible to be, at once, an absent lover, and happy too. For my part, I can meet with nothing that can please in the absence of Damon;

but on the contrary I see all things with disgust. I will flatter myself that it is so with you; and that the least evils appear great misfortunes; and that all those who speak to you of anything but of what you love increase your pain by a new remembrance of her absence. I will believe that these are your sentiments, when you are assured not to see me in some weeks; and if your heart do not betray your words, all those days will be tedious to you. I would not, however, have your melancholy too extreme; and to lessen it, you may persuade yourself that I partake it with you, for I remember in your last you told me you would wish we should be both grieved at the same time, and both at the same time pleased; and I believe I love too well not to obey you.

Love Secured

Love, of all joys, the sweetest is,
The most substantial happiness;
The softest blessing life can crave,
The noblest passion souls can have.
Yet, if no interruption were,
No difficulties came between,
'Twould not be rendered half so dear:
The sky is gayest when small clouds are seen.
The sweetest flower, the blushing rose,
Amidst the thorns securest grows.
If love were one continued joy,
How soon the happiness would cloy!
The wiser God did this foresee;
And to preserve the bliss entire,
Mixed it with doubt and jealousy,

Those necessary fuels to the fire;
Sustained the fleeting pleasures with new fears;
With little quarrels, sighs and tears;
With absence, that tormenting smart,
That makes a minute seem a day,
A day a year to the impatient heart,
That languishes in the delay,
But cannot sigh the tender pain away;
That still returns, and with a greater force,
Through every vein it takes its grateful course.
But whatsoe'er the lover does sustain,
Though he still sigh, complain, and fear;
It cannot be a mortal pain,
When two do the affliction bear.

TEN O'CLOCK
Reflections

After the afflicting thoughts of my absence, make some reflections on your happiness. Think it a blessing to be permitted to love me; think it so, because I permit it to you alone, and never could be drawn to allow it any other. The first thing you ought to consider is that at length I have suffered myself to be overcome, to quit that nicety that is natural to me, and receive your addresses; nay, thought them agreeable, and that I have at last confessed the present of your heart is very dear to me. It is true, I did not accept of it the first time it was offered me, nor before you had told me a thousand times that you could not escape expiring, if I did not give you leave to sigh for me, and gaze upon me; and that there was an absolute necessity for me either to give you leave to love or die. And all those rigours my severity has made you suffer ought now to be recounted to your memory as subjects of pleasure; and you ought to esteem and judge of the price of my affections by the difficulties you found in being able to touch my heart. Not but you have charms that can conquer at first sight; and you ought not to have valued me less if I had been more easily gained. But it is enough to please you, to think and know I am gained; no matter when and how. When, after a thousand cares and inquietudes, that which we wish for succeeds to our desires, the remembrance of those pains and pleasures we encountered in arriving at it gives us a new joy.

Remember also, Damon, that I have preferred you before all those that have been thought worthy of my esteem; and that I have shut my eyes to all their pleading merits, and could survey none but yours.

Consider then, that you had not only the happiness to please me, but that you only found out the way of doing it, and I had the goodness at last to tell you so, contrary to all the delicacy and niceness of my soul, contrary to my prudence, and all those scruples you know are natural to my humour.

My tenderness proceeded further, and I gave you innocent marks of my newborn passion, on all occasions that presented themselves. For, after that from my eyes and tongue you knew the sentiments of my heart, I confirmed that truth to you by my letters. Confess, Damon, that if you make these reflections, you will not pass this hour very disagreeably.

Beginning Love

As free as wanton winds I lived,
That unconcerned do play:
No broken faith, no fate I grieved;
No fortune gave me joy.
A dull content crowned all my hours,
My heart no sighs oppressed;
I call'd in vain on no deaf powers,
To ease a tortured breast.

The sighing swains regardless pined,
And strove in vain to please:
With pain I civilly was kind,
But could afford no ease.
Though wit and beauty did abound,
The charm was wanting still,
That could inspire the tender wound,
Or bend my careless will.

Till in my heart a kindling flame
Your softer sighs had blown;
Which I, with striving, love and shame,
Too sensibly did own.
Whate'er the god before could plead;
Whate'er the youth's desert;
The feeble siege in vain was laid
Against my stubborn heart.

At first my sighs and blushes spoke,
Just when your sighs would rise;

And when you gazed, I wished to look,
But durst not meet your eyes.
I trembled when my hand you pressed,
Nor could my guilt control;
But love prevailed, and I confessed
The secrets of my soul.

And when upon the giving part,
My present to avow,
By all the ways confirmed my heart,
That honour would allow;
Too mean was all that I could say,
Too poorly understood:
I gave my soul the noblest way,
My letters made it good.

You may believe I did not easily nor suddenly bring my
heart to this condescension; but I loved, and all things
in Damon were capable of making me resolve so to do.
I could not think it a crime where every grace, and every
virtue justified my choice. And when once one is assured
of this, we find not much difficulty in owning that passion
which will so well commend one's judgement; and there is
no obstacle that love does not surmount. I confessed
my weakness a thousand ways before I told it you; and
I remember all those things with pleasure, but yet I
remember them also with shame.

I will believe, Damon, that you have been so well entertained during this hour, and have found so much sweetness in these thoughts that if one did not tell you that supper waits, you would lose yourself in reflections so pleasing many more minutes. But you must go where you are expected; perhaps among the fair, the young, the gay; but do not abandon your heart to too much joy, though you have so much reason to be contented. But the greatest pleasures are always imperfect if the object beloved do not partake of it. For this reason be cheerful and merry with reserve. Do not talk too much, I know you do not love it; and if you do it, it will be the effect of too much complaisance, or with some design of pleasing too well; for you know your own charming power, and how agreeable your wit and conversation are to all the world. Remember, I am covetous of every word you speak that is not addressed to me, and envy the happy listener if I am not by. And I may reply to you as Amynta did to Philander when he charged her of loving a talker, and because, perhaps, you have not heard it, I will, to divert you, send it to you; and at the same time assure you, Damon, that your more noble quality, of speaking little, has reduced me to a perfect abhorrence of those wordy sparks that value themselves upon their ready and much talking upon every trivial subject, and who have so good an opinion of their talent that way, they will let nobody edge in a word or a reply but will make all the conversation themselves, that they may pass for very entertaining persons and pure company. But the verses –

The Reformation

Philander, since you'll have it so,
I grant I was impertinent;
And, till this moment, did not know,
Through all my life what 'twas I meant.
Your kind opinion was the flattering glass,
In which my mind found how deformed it was.

In your clear sense, which knows no art,
I saw the errors of my soul;
And all the foibles of my heart
With one reflection you control.
Kind as a god, and gently you chastise:
By what you hate, you teach me to be wise.

Impertinence, my sex's shame,
That has so long my life pursued,
You with such modesty reclaim,
As all the women has subdued.
To so divine a power what must I owe,
That renders me so like the perfect you?

That conversable thing I hate,
Already, with a just disdain,
That prides himself upon his prate,
And is, of words, that nonsense, vain:
When in your few appears such excellence
As have reproached and charmed me into sense.

For ever may I listening sit,
Though but each hour a word be born;
I would attend thy coming wit,
And bless what can so well inform.
Let the dull world henceforth to words be damned;
I'm into nobler sense than talking shamed.

I believe you are so good a lover as to be of my opinion; and that you will neither force yourself against nature nor find much occasion to lavish out those excellent things that must proceed from you, whenever you speak. If all women were like me, I should have more reason to fear your silence than your talk. For you have a thousand ways to charm without speaking, and those which to me show a great deal more concern. But, Damon, you know the greatest part of my sex judge the fine gentleman by the volubility of his tongue, by his dexterity in repartee, and cry, 'Oh! he never wants fine things to say. He's eternally talking the most surprising things.' But, Damon, you are well assured, I hope, that Iris is none of these coquettes. At least, if she had any spark of it once in her nature, she is by the excellency of your contrary temper taught to know and scorn the folly. And take heed your conduct never give me cause to suspect you have deceived me in your temper.

Nevertheless, Damon, civility requires a little complaisance after supper; and I am assured you can never want that, though, I confess, you are not accused of too general a complaisance, and do not often make use of it to those persons you have an indifference for, though one is not the less esteemable for having more of this than one ought; and though an excess of it be a fault, it is a very excusable one. Have therefore some for those with whom you are. You may laugh with them, drink with them, dance or sing with them; yet think of me. You may discourse of a thousand indifferent things with them, and at the same time still think of me. If the subject be any beautiful lady, whom they praise, either for her person, wit, or virtue, you may apply it to me. And if you dare not say it aloud, at least let your heart answer in this language:

> *Yes, the fair object, whom you praise*
> *Can give us love a thousand ways;*
> *Her wit and beauty charming are;*
> *But still my Iris is more fair.*

Nobody ever spoke before me of a faithful lover, but still I sighed and thought of Damon. And ever when they tell me tales of love, any soft pleasing intercourses of an amour, oh! with what pleasures do I listen! And with pleasure answer them, either with my eyes, or tongue –

> *That lover may his Sylvia warm,*

But cannot, like my Damon, charm.

If I have not all these excellent qualities you meet with in those beautiful people, I am however very glad that love prepossesses your heart to my advantage. And I need not tell you, Damon, that a true lover ought to persuade himself that all other objects ought to give place to her for whom his heart sighs. But see, my Cupid tells you it is one o'clock, and that you ought not to be longer from your apartment, where while you are undressing, I will give you leave to say to yourself –

The Regret

Alas! and must the sun decline,
Before it has informed my eyes
Of all that's glorious, all that's fine,
Of all I sigh for, all I prize?
How joyful were those happy days,
When Iris spread her charming rays,
Did my unwearied heart inspire
With never-ceasing awful fire,
And every minute gave me new desire!
But now, alas! all dead and pale,
Like flow'rs that wither in the shade:
Where no kind sunbeams can prevail,
To raise its cold and fading head,
I sink into my useless bed.
I grasp the senseless pillow as I lie;
A thousand times, in vain, I sighing cry,
Ah! would to Heaven my Iris were as nigh.

ONE O'CLOCK
Impossibility to Sleep

You have been up long enough; and Cupid, who takes care of your health, tells you it is time for you to go to bed. Perhaps you may not sleep as soon as you are laid, and possibly you may pass an hour in bed before you shut your eyes. In this impossibility of sleeping, I think it very proper for you to imagine what I am doing where I am. Let your fancy take a little journey then, invisible, to observe my actions and my conduct. You will find me sitting alone in my cabinet (for I am one that does not love to go to bed early) and will find me very uneasy and pensive, pleased with none of those things that so well entertain others. I shun all conversation, as far as civility will allow, and find no satisfaction like being alone, where my soul may, without interruption, converse with Damon. I sigh, and sometimes you will see my cheeks wet with tears that insensibly glide down at a thousand thoughts that present themselves soft and afflicting. I partake of all your inquietude. On other things I think with indifference, if ever my thoughts do stray from the more agreeable object. I find, however, a little sweetness in this thought, that, during my absence, your heart thinks of me, when mine sighs for you. Perhaps I am mistaken, and that at the same time that you are the entertainment of all my thoughts, I am no more in yours; and perhaps you are thinking of those things that immortalise the young and brave, either by those glories the muses flatter you with, or that of Bellona[10], and the god of war; and serving now a monarch, whose glorious acts in arms has outgone[11] all the feigned and real heroes of any age, who has, himself, outdone whatever history can produce of great and brave, and set so illustrious an example to the underworld that it is not impossible, as much a lover as you are, but you are thinking now how to render yourself worthy the glory of such a godlike master, by projecting a thousand things of gallantry and danger. And though, I confess, such thoughts are proper for your youth, your quality, and the place you have the honour to hold under our sovereign, yet let me tell you, Damon, you will not be without inquietude, if you think of either being a delicate poet, or a brave warrior; for love will still interrupt your glory, however you may think to divert him either by writing or fighting. And you ought to remember these verses:

Love and Glory

Beneath the kind protecting laurel's shade,
For sighing lovers and for warriors made,
The soft Adonis and rough Mars were laid.

Both were designed to take their rest;
But love the gentle boy oppressed,
And false alarms shook the stern hero's breast.

This thinks to soften all his toils of war,
In the dear arms of the obliging fair;
And that, by hunting, to divert his care.

All day, o'er hills and plains, wild beasts he chased,
Swift as the flying winds, his eager haste;
In vain, the god of love pursues as fast.

But oh! no sports, no toils divertive prove,
The evening still returns him to the grove,
To sigh and languish for the queen of love:

Where elegies and sonnets he does frame,
And to the listening echoes sighs her name,
And on the trees carves records of his flame.

The warrior in the dusty camp all day
With rattling drums and trumpets, does essay
To fright the tender flattering god away.

But still, alas, in vain: whate'er delight,
What cares he takes the wanton boy to fright,
Love still revenges it at night.

'Tis then he haunts the royal tent,
The sleeping hours in sighs are spent,
And all his resolutions does prevent.

In all his pains, Love mixed his smart;
In every wound he feels a dart;
And the soft god is trembling in his heart.

Then he retires to shady groves,
And there, in vain, he seeks repose,
And strives to fly from what he cannot lose.

While thus he lay, Bellona came,
And with a gen'rous fierce disdain,
Upbraids him with his feeble flame.

'Arise, the world's great terror, and their care;
Behold the glittering host from far,
That waits the conduct of the god of war.

'Beneath these glorious laurels, which were made
To crown the noble victor's head,
Why thus supinely art thou laid?

'Why on that face, where awful terror grew,
Thy sun-parched cheeks why do I view
The shining tracks of falling tears bedew?

'What god has wrought these universal harms?
What fatal nymph, what fatal charms,
Has made the hero deaf to war's alarms?

'Now let the conqu'ring ensigns up be furled:
Learn to be gay, be soft, and curled;
And idle lose the empire of the world.

'In fond effeminate delights go on;
Lose all the glories you have won:
Bravely resolve to love and be undone.'

'Tis thus the martial virgin pleads;
Thus she the amorous god persuades
To fly from Venus, and the flowery meads.

You see here that poets and warriors are oftentimes in affliction, even under the shades of their protecting laurels; and let the nymphs and virgins sing what they please to their memory, under the myrtles, and on flowery beds, they are much better days than in the campaign. Nor do the crowns of glory surpass those of love. The first is but an empty name, which is now kept and lost with hazard; but love more nobly employs a brave soul, and all his pleasures are solid and lasting; and when one has a worthy object of one's flame, glory accompanies love too. But go to sleep, the hour is come; though it is now that your soul ought to be entertained in dreams.

TWO O'CLOCK
Conversation in Dreams

I doubt not but you will think it very bold and arbitrary that my watch should pretend to rule even your sleeping hours, and that my Cupid should govern your very dreams, which are but thoughts disordered, in which reason has no part; chimeras of the imagination and no more. But though my watch does not pretend to counsel unreasonable, yet you must allow it here, if not to pass the bounds, at least to advance to the utmost limits of it. I am assured that, after having thought so much of me in the day, you will think of me also in the night. And the first dream my watch permits you to make, is to think you are in conversation with me.

Imagine, Damon, that you are talking to me of your passion with all the transport of a lover, and that I hear you with satisfaction; that all my looks and blushes, while you are speaking, give you new hopes and assurances; that you are not indifferent to me, and that I give you a thousand testimonies of my tenderness, all innocent and obliging.

While you are saying all that love can dictate, all that wit and good manners can invent, and all that I wish to hear from Damon, believe in this dream, all flattering and dear, that after having showed me the ardour of your flame, I confess to you the bottom of my heart, and all the loving secrets there; that I give you sigh for sigh, tenderness for tenderness, heart for heart, and pleasure for pleasure. And I would have your sense of this dream so perfect, and your joy so entire, that if it happen you should awake with the satisfaction of this dream, you should find your heart still panting with the soft pleasure of the dear deceiving transport, and you should be ready to cry out,

> *Ah! how sweet it is to dream,*
> *When charming Iris is the theme!*

For such, I wish, my Damon, your sleeping and your waking thoughts should render me to your heart.

THREE O'CLOCK
Capricious Suffering in Dreams

It is but just to mix a little chagrin with these pleasures, a little bitter with your sweet; you may be cloyed with too long an imagination of my favours. And I will have your fancy in dreams represent me to it as the most capricious maid in the world. I know, here you will accuse my watch, and blame me with unnecessary cruelty, as you will call it: but lovers have their little ends, their little advantages to pursue by methods wholly unaccountable to all but that heart which contrives them. And as good a lover as I believe you, you will not enter into my design at first sight, and though on reasonable thoughts you will be satisfied with this conduct of mine, at its first approach you will be ready to cry out –

The Request

Oh Iris! let my sleeping hours be fraught
With joys which you deny my waking thought.
Is't not enough you absent are?
Is't not enough I sigh all day,
And languish out my life in care,
To every passion made a prey?
I burn with love and soft desire;
I rave with jealousy and fear:
All day, for ease, my soul I tire;
In vain I search it everywhere:
It dwells not with the witty or the fair.

It is not in the camp or court,
In business, music, or in sport;
The plays, the park, the mall afford
No more than the dull basset-board[12].
The beauties in the drawing room,
With all their sweetness, all their bloom,
No more my faithful eyes invite,

Nor rob my Iris of a sigh or glance,
Unless soft thoughts of her incite
A smile, or trivial complaisance.
Then since my days so anxious prove,
Ah, cruel tyrant! give
A little loose to joys in love,
And let your Damon live.

Let him in dreams be happy made,
And let his sleep some bliss provide:
The nicest maid may yield in night's dark shade
What she so long by daylight had denied.
There let me think you present are,
And court my pillow for my fair.
There let me find you kind, and that you give
All that a man of honour dares receive.
And may my eyes eternal watches keep,
Rather than want that pleasure when I sleep.

Some such complaint as this I know you will make; but, Damon, if the little quarrels of lovers render the reconciling moments so infinitely charming, you must needs allow that these little chagrin in capricious dreams must awaken you to more joy to find them but dreams than if you had met with no disorder there. It is for this reason that I would have you suffer a little pain for a coming pleasure; nor indeed is it possible for you to escape the dreams my Cupid points you out. You shall dream that I have a thousand foibles, something of the lightness of my sex; that my soul is employed in a thousand vanities; that (proud and fond of lovers) I make advances for the glory of a slave without any other interest or design than that of being adored. I will give you leave to think my heart fickle, and that, far from resigning it to anyone, I lend it only for a day, or an hour, and take it back at pleasure; that I am a very coquette, even to impertinence.

All this I give you leave to think, and to offend me, but it is in sleep only that I permit it, for I would never pardon you the least offence of this nature, if in any other kind than in a dream. Nor is it enough affliction to you to imagine me thus idly vain, but you are to pass on to a hundred more capricious humours, as that I exact of you a hundred unjust things; that I pretend you should break off with all your friends, and for the future have none at all; that I will myself do those things which I violently condemn in you; and that I will have for others, as well as you, that tender friendship that resembles love, or rather love which people call friendship; and that I will not, after all, have you dare complain of me.

In fine, be as ingenious as you please to torment your-self and believe that I am become unjust, ungrateful, and insensible. But were I so indeed, O Damon! consider your awaking heart and tell me, would your love stand the proof of all the faults in me? But know that I would have you believe I have none of these weaknesses, though I am not wholly without faults, but those will be excusable to a lover, and this notion I have of a perfect one:

Whate'er fantastic humours rule the fair,
She's still the lover's dotage, and his care.

FOUR O'CLOCK
Jealousy in Dreams

Do not think, Damon, to wake yet, for I design you shall yet suffer a little more. Jealousy must now possess you, that tyrant over the heart that compels your very reason and seduces all your good nature. And in this dream you must believe that in sleeping, which you could not do me the injustice to do when awake. And here you must explain all my actions to the utmost disadvantage. Nay I will wish that the force of this jealousy may be so extreme that it may make you languish in grief, and be overcome with anger.

You shall now imagine that one of your rivals is with me, interrupting all you say, or hindering all you would say; that I have no attention to what you say aloud to me, but that I incline mine ear to hearken to all that he whispers to me. You shall repine[13] that he pursues me everywhere and is eternally at your heels if you approach me, that I caress him with sweetness in my eyes and that vanity in my heart that possesses the humours of almost all the fair that is, to believe it greatly for my glory to have abundance of rivals for my lovers. I know you love me too well not to be extremely uneasy in the company of a rival, and to have one perpetually near me; for let him be beloved or not by the mistress, it must be confessed, a rival is a very troublesome person. But to afflict you to the utmost, I will have you imagine that my eyes approve of all his thoughts; that they flatter him with hopes; and that I have taken away my heart from you to make a present of it to this more lucky man. You shall suffer, while possessed with this dream, all that a cruel jealousy can make a tender soul suffer.

The Torment

O Jealousy! Thou passion most ingrate!
Tormenting as despair, envious as hate!
Spiteful as witchcraft, which the invoker harms;
Worse than the wretch that suffers by its charms.
Thou subtle poison in the fancy bred,
Diffused through every vein, the heart and head,
And over all, like wild contagion spread.
Thou, whose sole property is to destroy,
Thou opposite to good, antipathy to joy;
Whose attributes are cruel rage and fire,
Reason debauched, false sense, and mad desire.

In fine, it is a passion that ruffles all the senses and disorders the whole frame of nature. It makes one hear and see what was never spoke, and what never was in view. It is the bane of health and beauty, an unmannerly intruder; and an evil of life worse than death. She is a very cruel tyrant in the heart; she possesses and pierces it with infinite unquiets; and we may lay it down as a certain maxim –

She that would rack a lover's heart
To the extent of cruelty,
Must his tranquillity pervert
To the most torturing jealousy.

I speak too sensibly of this passion not to have loved well enough to have been touched with it. And you shall be this unhappy lover, Damon, during this dream, in which nothing shall present itself to your tumultuous thoughts that shall not bring its pain. You shall here pass and re-pass a hundred designs that shall confound one another. In fine, Damon, anger, hatred and revenge shall surround your heart.

> *There they shall all together reign*
> *With mighty force, with mighty pain;*
> *In spite of reason, in contempt of love:*
> *Sometimes by turns, sometimes united move.*

FIVE O'CLOCK
Quarrels in Dreams

I perceive you are not able to suffer all this injustice, nor can I permit it any longer, and though you commit no crime yourself, yet you believe in this dream that I complain of the injuries you do my fame; and that I am extremely angry with a jealousy so prejudicial to my honour. Upon this belief you accuse me of weakness; you resolve to see me no more, and are making a thousand feeble vows against love. You esteem me as a false one, and resolve to cease loving the vain coquette, and will say to me as a certain friend of yours said to his false mistress:

> *The Inconstant*

> *Though, Sylvia, you are very fair,*
> *Yet disagreeable to me;*
> *And since you so inconstant are,*

79

Your beauty's damned with levity.
Your wit, your most offensive arms,
For want of judgement, wants its charms.

To every lover that is new,
All new and charming your surprise;
But when your fickle mind they view,
They shun the danger of your eyes.
Should you a miracle of beauty show,
Yet you're inconstant, and will still be so.

It is thus you will think of me. And in fine, Damon, during this dream, we are in perpetual state of war.

Thus both resolve to break their chain,
And think to do't without much pain,
But oh! alas! we strive in vain.
For lovers, of themselves, can nothing do;
There must be the consent of two:
You give it me, and I must give it you.

And if we shall never be free until we acquit one another, this tie between you and I, Damon, is likely to last as long as we live; therefore in vain you endeavour, but can never attain your end; and in conclusion you will say, in thinking of me:

Oh! how at ease my heart would live,
Could I renounce this fugitive;
This dear, but false, attracting maid,
That has her vows and faith betrayed!

Reason would have it so, but love
Dares not the dangerous trial prove.

Do not be angry then, for this afflicting hour is drawing to an end, and you ought not to despair of coming into my absolute favour again,

Then do not let your murmuring heart,
Against my interest, take your part.
The feud was raised by dreams, all false and vain,
And the next sleep shall reconcile again.

SIX O'CLOCK
Accommodation in Dreams

Though the angry lovers force themselves all they can to chase away the troublesome tenderness of the heart, in the height of their quarrels, love sees all their sufferings, pities and redresses them. And when we begin to cool, and a soft repentance follows the chagrin of the love quarrel, it is then that love takes the advantage of both hearts, and renews the charming friendship more forcibly than ever, puts a stop to all our feuds, and renders the peacemaking minutes the most dear and tender part of our life. How pleasing it is to see your rage dissolve! How sweet, how soft is every word that pleads for pardon at my feet! It is there that you tell me your very sufferings are overpaid, when I but assure you from my eyes that I will forget your crime. And your imagination shall here present me the most sensible of your past pain that you can wish; and that all my anger being banished, I give you a thousand marks of my faith and gratitude; and lastly, to crown all, that we again make new vows to one another of inviolable peace.

> *After these debates of love,*
> *Lovers thousand pleasures prove,*
> *Which they ever think to taste,*
> *Though oftentimes they do not last.*

Enjoy then all the pleasures that a heart that is very amorous, and very tender, can enjoy. Think no more on those inquietudes that you have suffered; bless love for his favours, and thank me for my graces, and resolve to endure anything, rather than enter upon any new quarrels. And however dear the reconciling moments are, there proceeds a great deal of evil from these little frequent quarrels; and I think the best counsel we can follow is to avoid them as near as we can. And if we cannot, but that, in spite of love and good understanding, they should break out, we ought to make as speedy peace as possible; for it is not good to grate the heart too long, lest it grow hardened insensibly and lose its native temper. A few quarrels there must be in love. Love cannot support itself without them, and besides the joy of an accommodation, love becomes by it more strongly united, and more charming. Therefore let the lover receive this as a certain receipt against declining love:

> *Love Reconciled*

> *He that would have the passion be*
> *Entire between the amorous pair,*

Let not the little feuds of jealousy
Be carried on to a despair:
That palls the pleasure he would raise;
The fire that he would blow, allays.
When understandings false arise,
When misinterpreted your thought,
If false conjectures of your smiles and eyes
Be up to baneful quarrels wrought;
Let love the kind occasion take,
And straight accommodations make.

The sullen lover, long unkind,
Ill-natured, hard to reconcile,
Loses the heart he had inclined;
Love cannot undergo long toil;
He's soft and sweet, not born to bear
The rough fatigues of painful war.

SEVEN O'CLOCK
Diverse Dreams

Behold, Damon, the last hour of your sleep, and of my watch. She leaves you at liberty now, and you may choose your dreams. Trust them to your imagination, give a loose to fancy, and let it rove at will, provided, Damon, it be always guided by a respectful love. For thus far I pretend to give bounds to your imagination, and will not have it pass beyond them. Take heed, in sleeping, you give no ear to a flattering Cupid, that will favour your slumbering minutes with lies too pleasing and vain.

You are discreet enough when you are awake; will you not be so in dreams?

Damon, awake; my watch's course is done; after this, you cannot be ignorant of what you ought to do during my absence. I did not believe it necessary to caution you about balls and comedies; you know a lover, deprived of his mistress, goes seldom there. But if you cannot handsomely avoid these diversions, I am not so unjust a mistress to be angry with you for it; go, if civility or other duties oblige you. I will only forbid you, in consideration of me, not to be too much satisfied with those pleasures; but see them so as the world may have reason to say you do not seek them; you do not make a business or pleasure of them; and that it is complaisance, and not inclination, that carries you thither. Seem rather negligent than concerned at anything there; and let every part of you say, 'Iris is not here –'

I say nothing to you neither of your duty elsewhere; I am satisfied you know it too well; and have too great a veneration for your glorious master to neglect any part of that for even love itself. And I very well know how much you love to be eternally near his illustrious person; and that you scarce prefer your mistress before him, in point of love. In all things else, I give him leave to take place of Iris in the noble heart of Damon.

I am satisfied you pass your time well now at Windsor, for you adore that place; and it is not, indeed, without great reason, for it is most certainly now rendered the most glorious palace in the Christian world. And had our late gracious sovereign, of blessed memory, had no other miracles and wonders of his life and reign to have immortalised his fame (of which there shall remain a thousand to posterity) this noble structure alone, this building (almost divine) would have eternised the great name of glorious Charles II[14] till the world moulder again to its old confusion, its first chaos. And the painting of the famous Varrio, and noble carvings of the inimitable Gibbon, shall never die, but remain to tell succeeding ages that all arts and learning were not confined to ancient Rome and Greece, but that England too could boast its mightiest share. Nor is the inside of this magnificent structure, immortalised with so many eternal images of the illustrious Charles and Catherine[15], more to be admired than the wondrous prospects without. The stupendous height, on which the famous pile is built renders the fields and flowery meadows below, the woods, the thickets, and the winding streams, the more delightful object that ever nature produced. Beyond all these and far below, in an inviting vale, the venerable college, an old, but noble building raises itself, in the midst of all the beauties of nature, high-grown trees, fruit-ful plains, purling rivulets, and spacious gardens, adorned with all variety of sweets that can delight the senses.

At further distance yet, on an ascent almost as high as that to the royal structure, you may behold the famous and noble Clifdon Rise, a palace erected by the illustrious Duke of Buckingham[16], who will leave this wondrous piece of architecture to inform the future world of the greatness and delicacy of his mind; it being for its situation, its prospects, and its marvellous contrivances, one of the finest villas of the world, at least, were it finished as begun; and would sufficiently declare the magnific soul of the hero that caused it to be built, and contrived all its fineness. And this makes up not the least part of the beautiful prospect from the Palace Royal, while on the other side lies spread a fruitful and delightful park and forest well stored with deer, and all that makes the prospect charming; fine walks, groves, distant valleys, downs and hills, and all that nature could invent to furnish out a quiet soft retreat for the most fair and most charming of queens, and the most heroic, good, and just of kings, and these groves alone are fit and worthy to divert such earthly gods.

Nor can heaven, nature, or human art contrive an addition to this earthly paradise, unless those great inventors of the age, Sir Samuel Moreland or Sir Robert Gordon[17], could by the power of engines convey the water so into the park and castle as to furnish it with delightful fountains, both useful and beautiful. These are only wanting to render the place all perfection, and without exception.

This, Damon, is a long digression from the business of my heart; but you know I am so in love with that charming court that when you gave me an occasion, by your being there now, only to name the place, I could not forbear transgressing a little in favour of its wondrous beauty; and the rather, because I would, in recounting it, give you to understand how many fine objects there are, besides the ladies that adorn it, to employ your vacant moments in; and I hope you will, without my instructions, pass a great part of your idle time in surveying these prospects, and give that admiration you should pay to living beauty, to those more venerable monuments of everlasting fame.

Neither need I, Damon, assign you your waiting times.

Your honour, duty, love, and obedience, will instruct you when to be near the person of the King; and I believe you will omit no part of that devoir. You ought to establish your fortune and your glory, for I am not of the mind of those critical lovers who believe it a very hard matter to reconcile love and interest, to adore a mistress and serve a master at the same time. And I have heard those, who on this subject, say, 'Let a man be never so careful in these double duties, it is ten to one but he loses his fortune or his mistress.' These are errors that I condemn. And I know that love and ambition are not incompatible, but that a brave man may preserve all his duties to his sovereign, and his passion and his respect for his mistress. And this is my notion of it.

Love and Ambition

The nobler lover, who would prove
Uncommon in address,
Let him ambition join with love;
With glory, tenderness:
But let the virtues so be mixed,
That when to love he goes,
Ambition may not come betwixt,
Nor love his power oppose.
The vacant hours from softer sport,
Let him give up to interest and the Court.

'Tis honour shall his business be,
And love his noblest play,
Those two should never disagree,

87

For both make either gay.
Love without honour were too mean
For any gallant heart;
And honour singly, but a dream,
Where love must have no part.
A flame like this you cannot fear,
Where glory claims an equal share.

Such a passion, Damon, can never make you quit any part
of your duty to your prince. And the monarch you serve is
so gallant a master that the inclination you have to his
person obliges you to serve him, as much as your duty;
for Damon's loyal soul loves the man, and adores the
monarch, for he is certainly all that compels both, by a
charming force and goodness, from all mankind.

   The King

Darling of Mars! Bellona's care!
The second deity of war!
Delight of heaven, and joy of earth!
Born for great and wondrous things,
Destined at his auspicious birth
To outdo the numerous race of long-past kings.

Best representative of heaven,
To whom its chiefest attributes are given!
Great, pious, steadfast, just, and brave!
To vengeance slow, but swift to save!
Dispensing mercy all abroad!
Soft and forgiving as a god!

Thou saving angel who preservest the land
From the just rage of the avenging hand;
Stopped the dire plague, that o'er the Earth
    was unjustly hurl'd,
And sheathing thy almighty sword,
Calmed the wild fears of a distracted world,
(As heaven first made it) with a sacred word!

But I will stop the low flight of my humble muse, who when she is upon the wing on this glorious subject, knows no bounds. And all the world has agreed to say so much of the virtues and wonders of this great monarch that they have left me nothing new to say; though indeed he every day gives us new themes of his growing greatness, and we see nothing that equals him in our age. Oh! how happy are we to obey his laws; for he is the greatest of kings, and the best of men!

You will be very unjust, Damon, if you do not confess I have acquitted myself like a maid of honour of all the obligations I owe you upon the account of the discretion I lost to you. If it be not valuable enough, I am generous enough to make it good. And since I am so willing to be just, you ought to esteem me, and to make it your chiefest care to preserve me yours; for I believe I shall deserve it, and wish you should believe so too. Remember me, write to me, and observe punctually all the motions of my watch. The more you regard it, the better you will like it; and whatever you think of it at first sight, it is no ill present. The invention is soft and gallant; and Germany, so celebrated for rare watches, can produce nothing to equal this.

Damon, my watch is just and new;
And all a lover ought to do,
My Cupid faithfully will show.
And every hour he renders there,
Except l'heure du Berger. [18]

NOTES

1. Aphra Behn's *The Lover's Watch* was based on *La Montre* (1666) by Balthazar de Bonnecorse (d.1706). Various editions of Behn's work exist; the Hesperus edition is based mainly on the revised version of 1735, with reference to other editions.

2. To make persistent demands for payment of a debt.

3. In this instance, meaning 'willing to please' rather than 'smugness'.

4. A writing desk.

5. Inferior in quality.

6. In Greek mythology, Thetis was the mother of Achilles, who she tried unsuccessfully to make immortal.

7. Venus' son refers to Cupid, the god of love; the Silenian god was Silenus, tutor to Dionysus, the god of wine.

8. To trick or deceive.

9. Deliberate or intentional.

10. In Greek mythology, Bellona was the goddess of war, and the wife of Mars.

11. To surpass.

12. Basset was an early version of the card-game faro.

13. To be discontented; fret.

14. Charles II (1630–85), died a year before the first publication of *The Lover's Watch*; Aphra Behn was rumoured to be his mistress. Charles was succeeded by his son, James II, who reigned until 1688.

15. Charles II's wife, Catherine of Braganza (1638–1705) was a Portuguese princess whom he married for her large dowry.

16. George Villiers, the second Duke of Buckingham (1627–87), was a favourite at the Court of Charles II.

17. Samuel Moreland (1625–95) was an inventor, interested mainly in hydraulics. In 1681 he was appointed master of mechanics to the King, for raising water from the Thames to Windsor Palace using a steam pump; Sir Robert Gordon is now remembered for building Gordonstoun House, the site of Gordonstoun School in Scotland.

18. The shepherd's hour, i.e. the lover's hour, the hour of tryst or the critical time.

Aphra Behn (née Johnson) was born in 1640 and baptised in Harbledon, just outside Canterbury. In 1663 she visited Surinam, then a British colony, with her family. On her return to England in 1664 she married Behn, a city merchant of Dutch extraction. The marriage was short-lived, and he is thought to have died a year later. In 1666 Aphra Behn served as a spy for Charles II in Antwerp, codenamed 'Astrea' or Agent 160. She was also rumoured to be Charles' mistress. A year later she was sent to debtors' prison for debts she incurred in the service of the Crown. It is likely that she was released shortly afterwards.

When her career as a professional spy came to an end, Behn became England's first professional writer. After Dryden, she was the most prolific dramatist of the Restoration period, and for the first twenty years of her career she was the only female playwright. Her first play, *The Forced Marriage*, was produced in 1670 at Lincoln's Inn Fields and proved a great success. This was followed by *The Amorous Prince* in 1671, *The Dutch Lover* in 1673 (not published until 1677), and *Abdelazer and The Town Fop*, also published in 1677. *The Rover*, perhaps Behn's most successful play, was produced in 1677 with Nell Gwyn playing the role of the whore Angelica Bianca. Other plays in the period 1678–81 include *Sir Patient Fancy*, *The Feigned Courtesans*, *The Young King*, *The False Count* and *The Roundheads*. *The City Heiress*, a satiric comedy of London life, produced in 1682, was followed by *Like Father, Like Son*, which was such a failure that it was never published and has since been lost. Behn was then arrested for writing an 'abusive' prologue but was probably let off with a warning.

In 1683 Behn published the first part of *Love Letters between a Nobleman and his Sister*, the first major epistolary novel in English literature. She also wrote poetry, with *Poems on Several Occasions* appearing in 1684, and *Miscellany* a year later. *The Lover's Watch* was published in 1686, followed by *The Lucky Chance*, Behn's first play since the failure of *Like Father, Like Son*. It explores one of her favourite themes, namely the dire consequences of arranged and ill-matched marriages. In 1688 three prose works by Aphra Behn were published including her most famous work, *Oroonoko*, based on her time in Surinam. Fiercely critical of the slave trade, *Oroonoko* is perhaps the earliest English philosophical novel.

Aphra Behn died on 16th April 1689 and is buried in Westminster Abbey. Two of her plays, *The Widow Ranter* and *The Younger Brother*, were produced posthumously. Virginia Woolf was later to write of her that, 'All women together ought to let flowers fall upon the tomb of Aphra Behn, for it was she who earned them the right to speak their minds.'

HESPERUS PRESS CLASSICS

Hesperus Press, as suggested by the Latin motto, is committed to bringing near what is far – far both in space and time. Works written by the greatest authors, and unjustly neglected or simply little known in the English-speaking world, are made accessible through new translations and a completely fresh editorial approach. Through these classic works, the reader is introduced to the greatest writers from all times and all cultures.

For more information on Hesperus Press, please visit our website: **www.hesperuspress.com**

ET REMOTISSIMA PROPE

SELECTED TITLES FROM HESPERUS PRESS

Author	Title	Foreword writer
Louisa May Alcott	*Behind a Mask*	Doris Lessing
Pedro Antonio de Alarcon	*The Three-Cornered Hat*	
Pietro Aretino	*The School of Whoredom*	Paul Bailey
Jane Austen	*Love and Friendship*	Fay Weldon
Honoré de Balzac	*Colonel Chabert*	A.N. Wilson
Charles Baudelaire	*On Wine and Hashish*	Margaret Drabble
Giovanni Boccaccio	*Life of Dante*	A.N. Wilson
Charlotte Brontë	*The Green Dwarf*	Libby Purves
Mikhail Bulgakov	*The Fatal Eggs*	Doris Lessing
Giacomo Casanova	*The Duel*	Tim Parks
Miguel de Cervantes	*The Dialogue of the Dogs*	
Anton Chekhov	*The Story of a Nobody*	Louis de Bernières
Anton Chekhov	*Three Years*	William Fiennes
Wilkie Collins	*Who Killed Zebedee?*	Martin Jarvis
Arthur Conan Doyle	*The Tragedy of the Korosko*	Tony Robinson
William Congreve	*Incognita*	Peter Ackroyd
Joseph Conrad	*Heart of Darkness*	A.N. Wilson
Joseph Conrad	*The Return*	Colm Tóibín
Gabriele D'Annunzio	*The Book of the Virgins*	Tim Parks
Dante Alighieri	*New Life*	Louis de Bernières
Daniel Defoe	*The King of Pirates*	Peter Ackroyd
Marquis de Sade	*Incest*	Janet Street-Porter
Charles Dickens	*A House to Let*	
Charles Dickens	*The Haunted House*	Peter Ackroyd
Fyodor Dostoevsky	*The Double*	Jeremy Dyson
Fyodor Dostoevsky	*Poor People*	Charlotte Hobson
Joseph von Eichendorff	*Life of a Good-for-nothing*	
George Eliot	*Amos Barton*	Matthew Sweet
Henry Fielding	*Jonathan Wild the Great*	